This edition published by Parragon Books Ltd in 2016

Parragon Books Ltd
Chartist House
15–17 Trim Street
Bath BA1 1HA, UK
www.parragon.com

ISBN 978-1-4748-3293-9

Printed in China

Bath • New York • Cologne • Melbourne • Delhi
Hong Kong • Shenzhen • Singapore

The kingdom of Arendelle was a happy place, located next to a deep fjord. At night, the Northern Lights often lit up the skies in beautiful patterns. But the king and queen lived with a secret worry.

Their eldest daughter, Elsa, had magical powers.
She could freeze things and create snow, even
in summer!

Their youngest daughter, Anna, adored her older
sister. The two loved to play together in the snowy
playgrounds that Elsa created.

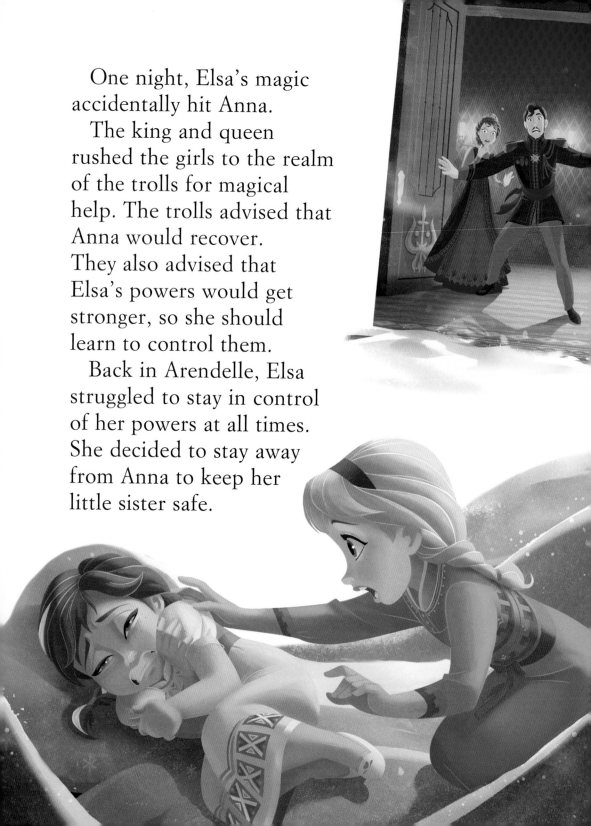

One night, Elsa's magic accidentally hit Anna.

The king and queen rushed the girls to the realm of the trolls for magical help. The trolls advised that Anna would recover. They also advised that Elsa's powers would get stronger, so she should learn to control them.

Back in Arendelle, Elsa struggled to stay in control of her powers at all times. She decided to stay away from Anna to keep her little sister safe.

The trolls had changed Anna's memories, so she didn't remember Elsa's magic. She grew up thinking that Elsa wanted nothing to do with her.

By the time Elsa was crowned queen, the sisters had grown apart. They hardly knew each other.

Having grown up mostly by herself, Anna had felt lonely for a long time. So she was thrilled to meet handsome Prince Hans on the day of Elsa's coronation.

Anna and Hans liked each other right away. At the coronation party they danced and talked all night.

Anna thought it was a great idea to get engaged quickly. But Elsa reacted angrily, "How can you marry someone you've just met?"

Anna argued back. "I can't live like this any more!"

Then Elsa got upset and an icy blast shot from her hand – in front of everyone!

Worried that her secret was exposed, and afraid she would hurt someone, Elsa fled from the castle. Everything froze behind her as she ran away.

Once Elsa climbed into the mountains she calmed down. All alone, she was able to let her powers out, for the first time ever! She created whirls of snow, ice and even an ice palace.

She was able to be herself and it felt wonderful!

Meanwhile, Anna realized that Elsa had been acting distant for all those years because she had had to hide her magic. Anna decided to go after Elsa – now that her secret was out, they could be together!

Anna headed up the mountain, but her horse threw her into the snow. Luckily, she was able to find shelter in a nearby shop.

Inside, Anna met a young man covered in frost. He was cross because he was an ice harvester and the mid-summer snowstorm was ruining his business.

He also knew where the storm was coming from. That meant he could take her to Elsa!

Anna hired the young man, who was called Kristoff, to take her up the North Mountain to find Elsa. His reindeer, Sven, came along, too.

As they neared the top of the mountain, the trio saw a beautiful wintery landscape. Elsa had covered everything with colourful, sparkling ice.

Elsa had also created a snowman ... who was alive!

The snowman's name was Olaf and he was excited to hear that Anna planned to bring back summer, because he loved the idea of warm weather.

He volunteered to take them to Elsa.

As the group continued on they found the fantastic ice palace that Elsa had created with her magic.

Anna was impressed by Elsa's powers and her ice palace. But she wanted Elsa to come home. Elsa thought the people of Arendelle wouldn't accept her – and she was still afraid of hurting them. The two girls argued.

Although Elsa didn't intend to hurt Anna, she hit her sister in the chest with a blast of ice.

Then she created another snowman, named
Marshmallow, who was much bigger than Olaf.
The snowman made sure that Anna, Kristoff and
Olaf left the mountain quickly!

Once they were safe Kristoff noticed that Anna's hair was turning white. Kristoff took her to the trolls to see if their magic could help.

The trolls explained that Elsa's blast had hit Anna in the heart – and that soon she would freeze completely! But, they added, "An act of true love will thaw a frozen heart."

Olaf and Kristoff decided to hurry Anna back to Arendelle so she could get a true love's kiss from Hans.

Meanwhile, back in Arendelle, Hans helped everyone during the storm. Then Anna's horse returned to Arendelle without her!

Hans took a group out to find Anna ... but found Elsa first. Elsa was forced to defend herself against some of the men. Finally, she was taken back to Arendelle – as a prisoner! The men were convinced she was dangerous.

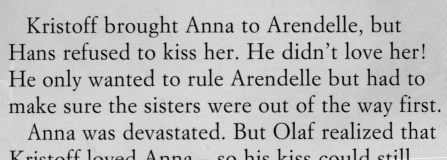

Kristoff brought Anna to Arendelle, but Hans refused to kiss her. He didn't love her! He only wanted to rule Arendelle but had to make sure the sisters were out of the way first.

Anna was devastated. But Olaf realized that Kristoff loved Anna – so his kiss could still save her. Anna made her way towards Kristoff. Then she saw her sister in danger....

She threw herself in front of Elsa, just in time to block a blow from Hans's sword.

At that moment, Anna transformed into solid ice. The sword shattered against her icy body.

Stunned, Elsa threw her arms round Anna and cried. She didn't want to lose her sister.

Suddenly, Anna began to melt. Anna's act of true love for her sister meant that the spell was broken!

Then, with Anna's love and faith, Elsa managed to bring back summer.

The sisters hugged and promised to love each other from then on. The people of Arendelle saw everything and they welcomed Elsa home.

Kristoff decided to stay in Arendelle and so did Olaf – with the help of a little winter cloud to keep him cool. Best of all, the sisters were back together and happy at last!